A PRESENT for ROSE

A PRESENT for ROSE

WRITTEN BY

Cooper Edens

ILLUSTRATED BY

Molly Hashimoto

SASQUATCH BOOKS

SEATTLE

Printed in China
Design and title by Judythe Sieck

Library of Congress Card Number 93-8398
ISBN 0-912365-89-7

Library of Congress
Cataloging in Publication
Data is available.

Distributed in Canada
by Raincoast Books
112 East Third Avenue
Vancouver, B.C. V5T 1C8

Sasquatch Books
1008 Western Avenue
Seattle, Washington 98104
(206) 467-4300

From
dream
to
dream
every
small
thing
changes
while
every
big
thing
stays
the
same.

With
the
last
days
of
winter
came
a
present
for
Rose.

Beautiful
as
the
present
was
Rose
wanted
to
know
what
it
contained.
She
never
guessed
when
she
pulled
the
ribbon
that
she
would
end
up
on
the
inside.

Rose
looked
around
and
discovered
a
door.
When
she
opened
it
sunlight
came
in.

Rose
walked
through
the
doorway
and
followed
a
path
to
another
present.
This
one
held
a
garden
and
the
first
day
of
spring.

Rose
opened
the
gate
and
went
far
into
the
garden.
Soon
she
was
standing
before
a
great
present
of
a
mountain.

Rose
crossed
the
field
and
approached
the
edge
of
the
mountain
where
she
came
upon
a
waterfall.
She
thought
it
strange
that
the
waterfall
had
been
wrapped
up-
side
down.

So
Rose
turned
the
waterfall
right
side
up.

On
the
last
day
of
spring
Rose
walked
to
the
falls
and
saw
a
present
with
a
table
and
a
chair
floating
inside
it.

Rose
dove
for
the
chair.
She
was
feeling
tired
from
her
journey
and
wished
to
sit
down.

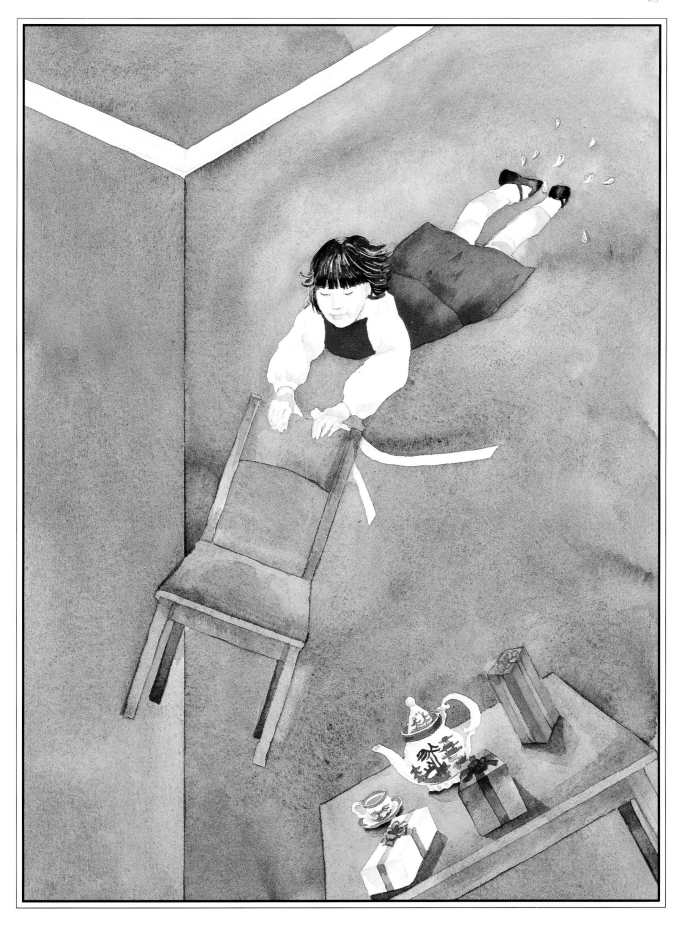

On
the
table
there
was
a
pot
of
tea
a
cup
and
three
lovely
presents
that
Rose
was
happy
to
open.

One
was
the
summer
sun
the
second
the
summer
moon
and
the
third
the
summer
stars.

Rose
watched
the
sun
the
moon
and
the
stars
rise.
She
leaned
so
far
from
the
table
that
she
tumbled
over
backwards...

. . . and
landed
in
the
soft
grass
of
the
first
day
of
autumn.

AUTHOR'S NOTE

*I have based my poem "A Present for Rose" on a traditional folktale told
among the Japanese, offering the philosophy that each of the seasons
is a present to humanity and within that present you will always
find the next season.
To this I have added another Japanese tradition, a belief that all heavenly
bodies (stars, planets, moons, and comets) were once presents, and that today,
by opening gifts, we continue to create the universe.
I hope that this poem, inspired by a combination of folktales,
brings its readers delight.*

—Cooper Edens

Cooper Edens is the award-winning author and illustrator of
Caretakers of Wonder, The Starcleaner Reunion, and *If You Are Afraid
of the Dark, Remember the Night Rainbow.* He is the author of *Santa
Cows,* illustrated by Dan Lane. He lives in Seattle.

A Present for Rose is **Molly Hashimoto**'s first book. She lives in
Seattle with her family and a daughter named Rose.